MAGGIE SPARKS

Published by Sweet Cherry Publishing Limited
Unit 36, Vulcan House,
Vulcan Road,
Leicester, LE5 3EF
United Kingdom

First published in the US in 2022
2022 edition

2 4 6 8 10 9 7 5 3 1

ISBN: 978-1-78226-776-8

Maggie Sparks and the Monster Baby

Cover design by Esther Hernando and Rhiannon Izard
Illustrations by Esther Hernando

Lexile® code numerical measure L = Lexile® 620L

www.sweetcherrypublishing.com

Printed and bound in India
I.TP002

MAGGIE SPARKS

AND THE
MONSTER BABY

STEVE SMALLMAN

ILLUSTRATED BY
ESTHER HERNANDO

Sweet
Cherry

MAGGIE

That's me!

BAT

The coolest
chameleon
EVER.

MOM

Super smart.
Bakes great cookies.

DAD

Writes a lot.
Cannot bake cookies.

ALFIE
Stinky and annoying.

GRANDPA
My favorite
wizard in the world!

ARTHUR
My best friend.

CHAPTER 1

Maggie Sparks was a witch. A small, curly-haired, freckle-faced witch, who was usually full of mischief and fizzing with

MAGIC.

But not today. Today she was worried.

Grandpa Sparks, Maggie's favorite person in the whole world, was looking after her while Mom and Dad were away. She should have been as happy as a witch who'd worked out the secret to an excellent slime spell. But she wasn't.

Grandpa could see that Maggie was worried. Even Bat, her pet chameleon, had changed color to Worry White to match Maggie's mood.

"Don't worry," said Grandpa Sparks. "Mommy and Daddy will be home soon!"

"That's what I'm worried about!" cried Maggie.

Mom and Dad had gone to the hospital to swap Mom's big tummy for a baby. They'd been gone for AAAAAAAAGES.

"What do they want a baby for?" said Maggie. "What's the matter with me?"

"There's nothing the matter with you, Maggie Moo!" said Grandpa Sparks.

He gave her one of his warm, crinkly smiles. "But think what fun it will be to have a baby brother!"

"Can't I have a goldfish instead?" asked Maggie.

"Well, no," said Grandpa Sparks.

"But you'll be able to play with your brother."

"I could play with a goldfish," said Maggie.

"Yes, but one day," Grandpa Sparks went on, "you'll be able to do magic with your brother!"

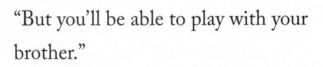

Maggie's eyes lit up.

"I can do magic on the baby?" she said with a grin. "Awesome! I could turn him into a goldfish!"

"No, no, not on him, with him!" said Grandpa Sparks.

"That's boring," grumbled Maggie.

"Just you wait, Maggie. As soon as you see him, you'll love him to bits."

Suddenly, a terrible screeching noise came from outside.

Was it a terrifying pterodactyl pouncing on Penny the mail carrier? Was it a tomcat with his tail trapped in a toilet seat?

No. It was Maggie's new baby brother.

Bat dived into the fruit bowl and disguised himself as a banana.

Seconds later, Mom and Dad marched through the door. They were smiling proudly and holding a screaming bundle.

"Look Maggie!" Dad shouted over the noise. "This is Alfie!"

Maggie looked down at the little noise monster. Its face was all red and wrinkly. It had no hair, no teeth and was covered in drool.

YUCK!

"What a beautiful baby boy!" said
Grandpa Sparks.

"Beautiful?" said Maggie. "He
looks like an angry potato! Why is
he making that noise?"

"He's just hungry," said Mom.
She gave Alfie his bottle.

As if by magic, the noise stopped.

"Is that magic milk?" asked Maggie.

"No," chuckled Dad. "It's Mommy milk."

Mommy milk? Maggie was confused. "But I thought milk only came from—"

"Cows?" suggested Dad.

"Fridges," said Maggie.

Then Dad propped Alfie over
his shoulder, patted his back and ...

BURRRRRP!

"Good boy!"
said Mom.

Maggie watched as everybody gazed down gooey-eyed at the baby. She had a funny feeling in her tummy. She felt worried and angry and sad all at the same time.

Bat turned bright green.

OH DEAR!

Maggie wasn't just worried and angry and sad; she was jealous too.

Bat could sense Maggie's magic was building. Her fingers began to tingle and tiny sparks started to fizz from her hair. Bat ducked further down into the fruit bowl.

Turning away from Mom and Dad, Maggie reached up her sleeve and pulled out her wand. She could make a much bigger burp than snotty baby Alfie. All she needed was a little MAGIC.

Maggie wiggled her wand and whispered:

"Wild wind blow and thunder roar, make my burp better than the one before!"

There was a short pause before,

"BUUUURRRRRRP!"

The curtains flapped. The floorboards rattled. The awful picture of Great Aunt Enid fell on the floor and Grandpa Sparks' hat blew right off his head!

It was the biggest burp that Maggie had ever burped. She waited to be told "Good girl!" and maybe even get a round of applause.

"Maggie!" gasped Dad.

"That was very rude!" said Mom.

The monster baby started crying again.

Grandpa Sparks just shook his head and picked up his hat.

Maggie sat scowling in the
"naughty corner," while Mom
rocked Alfie to sleep on the couch.
Bat climbed onto Maggie's shoulder
and licked her ear. It usually made
her laugh. But not today.

Maggie looked over her shoulder
at the tiny monster, now fast asleep
in her mom's arms.

"Maggie?" said Mom. "Would you
like to hold Alfie? You can come out
of the naughty corner and sit next

to me," she added, patting the couch cushion next to her.

"No," snapped Maggie. "I think he should go in his cage now."

"It's a crib, Maggie, not a cage," said Mom, as she stood up and laid the sleeping baby inside it.

"Well, I think I'd better leave you to it," said Grandpa Sparks, heaving himself up off the couch.

He kissed Mom, hugged Dad and stroked the monster's little head. Then he picked Maggie up and gave her a big cuddle.

"See you later, Maggie Moo," he said. Then he whispered in her ear,

"Brilliant burp!"

Maggie smiled and started to feel a bit happier.

The baby was behind bars (where it belonged!) and Mom had freed Maggie from the "naughty corner" a whole three minutes early.

Maggie looked at Alfie through the side of his crib. He looked less like a potato now. He was even smiling in his sleep. Maggie could feel the corners of her mouth start to curl up just a tiny bit before a loud

PARP

came from his diaper.

"Ew! We'll have to keep an eye on this one," Maggie whispered to Bat. "He's trouble!"

CHAPTER 2

Maggie had been right. Alfie was
trouble. Things only got worse as he
got bigger!

At first, he'd stayed where he was
put: in his crib or on his blanket.
But once the drooling monster
learned to crawl and climb and
pull himself up onto the furniture,
nothing was safe. Maggie had to
magic her things up onto the ceiling

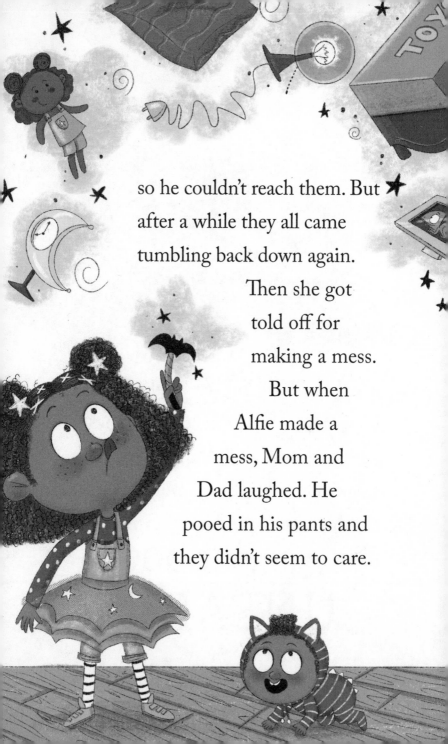

so he couldn't reach them. But
after a while they all came
tumbling back down again.
Then she got
told off for
making a mess.
But when
Alfie made a
mess, Mom and
Dad laughed. He
pooed in his pants and
they didn't seem to care.

He threw his breakfast on the floor,
blew raspberries at the dinner table,
chewed books and could empty a
tissue box in less than a minute.
But he never got told off!

IT WAS SOOOOOOO
UNFAIR!

Alfie even got to stay up late with Mom and Dad when Maggie was sent to bed. Everyone thought he was so wonderful. Everyone except Maggie.

One morning,
Mom and Maggie were
walking down the hill into
town. Maggie was pushing
Alfie's stroller. She was just
thinking how much faster the
stroller would get to the bottom of
the hill if she let go of it, when they
bumped into Penny the mail carrier.

As usual, Penny looked like she
was going to start complaining
about something. Then she suddenly
spotted Alfie and smiled. "Oh, what a
lovely little fella!" she said.

Later, in Mom's flower shop,
Mr. Battenberg from the bakery
saw Alfie through the window and
rushed in just to see him.

"Oh, aren't you adorable!" he
cooed. Then he looked around,
realized where he was and added,
"I'll have two bunches of daffodils
since I'm here, please Hetty!"

It was just as bad at the
supermarket! An old lady leaned
over, poked Alfie's tummy
with her wrinkled finger
and said, "Who's
this widdle dumply
wumply woo, then?"

Yes, everyone loved Alfie. And nobody seemed to notice Maggie at all.

Maggie started to feel strange.

Her toes began to tingle as they trudged back up the hill to their house. By the time they reached their garden gate, Maggie's feet felt so itchy that she pulled down her socks to scratch them.

But her feet had disappeared!

"MOM!" she cried. "MY FEET!"

"Yes, I know," said Mom, as she tried to stop Alfie from biting a hole in a box of coco puffs. "My feet are aching too. That hill seems to be getting steeper every day!"

"BUT MOM!"

Maggie tried again. She was interrupted by a loud squishing sound coming from the bottom end of Alfie. It was followed by a smell so bad it made Maggie's eyes water.

Mom carried Alfie into the house at arm's length to change his diaper.

Maggie sighed and went up to her room. She took off her shoes and socks. Oh no! Her feet really had disappeared. Then she lifted up her T-shirt. Oh dear! Her tummy wasn't there either. And now her arms were fading away too.

Maggie shut the door and quickly took off her clothes. She looked in the mirror and nearly fell over onto her invisible butt.

Only her head was left! It looked as if it were floating in mid-air!

Then, as she watched, her face went fuzzy around the edges. It started to lose color and then, suddenly, it disappeared altogether.

"Oh no!" Maggie cried. "I really am invisible!"

The shouting woke Bat, who had been dozing on his sleeping stick beside Maggie's bed.

"Oh Bat," Maggie said. "What am I going to do?"

Bat looked all around the room, which didn't take long because he could look in two directions at once. He could hear Maggie, but he definitely couldn't see her.

Maggie sniffed and wiped a tear from

her eye. "How am I going to comb my hair?" she said. "Or clean my teeth? Or do my homework?"

Then she remembered that she didn't like combing her hair or cleaning her teeth or doing her homework.

"If nobody can see me," Maggie said, "then nobody can see what I'm doing. Oh, this could be fun!"

Maggie fetched a white sheet from the closet and pulled it over her head. Then she tiptoed across the hallway to Dad's office.

She pushed the door open and let out a loud,

"WoooOooOoOOH!"

Dad nearly fell off his chair. His arm shot to the side and knocked a mug of coffee all over his desk.

"Maggie!" he said crossly. "I'm trying to work!" He walked across the room and snatched the sheet from her head.

But when he saw that there was nothing underneath the sheet, Dad's face turned very pale.

He gave a little squeak, dropped the sheet and ran downstairs.

"Are you alright, dear?" asked Mom. "You look like you've seen a ghost!"

"Just need t-t-to run to the doctors," he said, rubbing his forehead. "N-n-nothing to worry about, darling." Then he unlocked the door and walked quickly down the road, muttering to himself, "I must be seeing things. And hearing things. Maybe it's hunger. Or too much coffee. I need to cut down on the coffee."

Maggie was trying really hard not to giggle as she tiptoed down the stairs.

A lovely sweet, chocolatey smell was coming from the kitchen.

Alfie was strapped into his high chair and Mom was loading the dishwasher. A tray full of double chocolate-chip cookies were cooling on the table. Alfie was stretching his chubby little hands out to reach them, but Mom had made sure his high chair was too far away.

This was Maggie's chance. She stepped silently towards the table. She was only going to take a couple. But, wait … she had a brilliant idea!

What if Alfie stole the cookies? That would show Mom what the little monster was really like. Very quietly and verrrrrry slowly, Maggie pushed Alfie's high chair closer to the cookies.

With a squeal of delight, the
dribbly demon grabbed the corner of
the tray and flipped all the cookies
into the air.

"Alfie, no!" cried Mom, as cookies went everywhere.

Mom was so busy clearing up that she didn't notice when three cookies floated out of the door.

"YUM!" said Maggie, as she stood in the hallway scoffing down the chocolate-chip goodies.

She felt very pleased with herself.

"Oh Alfie," said Mom, sadly. "I made these cookies especially for Maggie, to cheer her up. Now they are all over the floor."

Maggie felt awful. Mom had been doing something nice, just for her!

Maggie started to feel warm all over. The more she felt as

though she mattered, the more visible she became. First her head appeared, then her shoulders, her tummy, her arms, her legs, her fingers and finally her ten little toes appeared like two rows of magic beans.

"I'm back!" said Maggie.

"Maggie!" cried Mom, looking out into the hallway. "What are you doing? Why haven't you got any clothes on?"

Maggie didn't know what to say. She turned and ran back to her bedroom to find some clothes.

CHAPTER 3

Maggie had just got dressed again when—

DING DONG!

She rushed downstairs to see who was at the door.

A small, scruffy-haired boy wearing glasses and a coat that was too big for him stood on the doorstep.

It was Maggie's best friend, Arthur.

Arthur wasn't a wizard or anything.

It's fair to say that there was
nothing magical about Arthur.

Right then he was staring at the
ground, looking worried. But then
Arthur usually looked worried.

He had a worried sort of face.

"Hello, Arthur. You will never believe the day I've had today!" said Maggie. "And it's all because of that little monster!"

"What little monster?" asked Arthur, looking around nervously.

Arthur never knew what to expect at Maggie's house. There could be a dragon in the dining room, a boogeyman in the bathroom or a troll in the toilet for all he knew!

"THAT MONSTER!" said Maggie as Alfie crawled into the hall.

Alfie looked up at Arthur, giggled and gave him a great big, two-toothed smile! Arthur smiled back at him, gave a little wave and said, "Hello Alfie!" in a silly, sing-song voice.

Maggie couldn't believe it!

"You traitor!" she shouted. "You're supposed to be my friend! But with one smile from that little pest, you go all smiley and gooey."

"But he's sooooooooooo cute," said Arthur. "Even if he is a pest. He's like a mouse."

"What are you talking about?" asked Maggie.

"Well," said Arthur, "some people think mice are pests, but some people think they're cute. I like mice, but not if they poop in your lunchbox. My uncle Norman had a mouse that pooed in his lunchbox once. He had a piece of chocolate cake in it and he thought the mouse poop was a bit of chocolate, so he ate it. But it didn't taste like chocolate, it tasted like mouse poop."

Maggie rolled her eyes.

"Goodbye Arthur," she said and closed the door.

"Er ... I'll be going then," Arthur shouted through the letter box. Then he shuffled back down the garden path.

Maggie stomped up to her bedroom and slammed the door.

Arthur had been no help and more annoyingly, he was right. Alfie was so stupidly cute!

"That's why he gets away with so much!" she told Bat. "He just has to flash a smile, pull a funny face or put a potty on his head and everyone melts.

"Oh, Bat," she sighed. "I must make myself cuter. Even cuter than a mouse who hasn't pooped in a lunch box!"

Maggie looked at herself in the mirror.

"What if I pull out my teeth?" she said. "Alfie only has two teeth. Would

I look cuter with just two teeth?"
Bat shook his head in panic.

"Hmm," Maggie said, opening
her pajama drawer. "I could start
wearing pajamas
all the time. And
nappies. Maybe
I should rub
yoghurt all over
my face?"

Bat shook his
head again.

"Well, if that will not work, then I suppose it's time for a little bit of magic!"

Maggie searched under the piles of clothes, toys and books scattered around her room.

"Bat, have you seen my wand?" she asked, with a stray sock draped over one ear.

Bat crossed his fingers behind his back and shook his head.

"Bat, did you hide my wand again?"

The chameleon blushed and looked down at his feet. Then he crawled under the bed.

There, in a jumble of coloring pencils,

half-eaten cookies and spilled potions, lay Maggie's wand. It was short, stripy, slightly bent and had a bat-shaped eraser stuck on the end.

Bat used his tail to pass the wand to Maggie, then quickly dived back under the bed.

Maggie wiggled her wand and chanted:

"Sweet as ice cream on a big bowl of fruit, magic please make me incredibly cute!"

POOF!

Maggie looked in the mirror and there, staring back at her, was a soft, floppy-eared bunny rabbit, with big brown eyes and a little pink heart-shaped nose.

"Noooooooo!" Maggie said—or tried to say. But no words came out.

This was not what she had meant!

She needed to cast another spell to fix this one. But she couldn't pick up her wand with her bunny paws. She couldn't say the words of a spell either, because she could only speak bunny (and bunnies hardly speak at all!).

I'll find Mom, thought Maggie. Maybe she can help.

Maggie jumped up at the door handle. After five tries, she managed to open the door. She hopped clumsily down the stairs with a worried little chameleon scuttling after her.

Maggie could hear Mom
talking on the phone. She
hopped towards the living
room. But before she got there
Alfie came crawling out into the hall.

"BUM BUM!" he said
excitedly, and tried to grab Maggie
by her fluffy tail.

Maggie jumped this way and that but she hadn't had much hopping practice, and Alfie could crawl at lightning speed. He grabbed Maggie and gave her a big squeeze.

"Aah," Alfie cooed.

Maggie tried to shout, "Get off!" But all that came out was a squeak.

Bat bravely darted forwards, stuck out his long tongue and tickled Alfie's ear with it. Alfie giggled, dropped Maggie and grabbed Bat instead!

Alfie gave Bat a big squeeze. Bat's tongue shot out and his curly tail straightened like a party horn. Alfie giggled. He was having a great time. Bat was not.

Thankfully, the front door opened, distracting the chameleon-squeezing monster.

"I'm home," said Dad, peeking around the door to check for imaginary ghosts. "Ok, no ghosts, that's good," he said, letting out a deep breath.

"Da-da?" said Alfie and dropped Bat on the floor.

Maggie hopped over to rescue Bat, who jumped onto her back like a cowboy.

"Bum bum!" cried Alfie, reaching for Maggie again. But with one mighty hop, Maggie shot towards Dad, slid through his legs and tumbled straight out of the front door.

Without even noticing the flying bunny, Dad scooped Alfie up one-handed and closed the door with his foot.

SLAM!

Maggie and Bat were locked out.

CHAPTER 4

Alfie started to cry.

"Bum bum!" he wailed.

"What's wrong with Alfie?" asked Dad. "Why does he keep shouting about his butt?"

"Oh!" said Mom, coming out into the hallway. "What a smart cookie! I expect he wants you to change his diaper. It seems you got home just in time."

Dad grumbled.

But even after his diaper had been changed, Alfie kept on crying. "Bum bum! BUM BUM!"

Dad handed him back to Mom. "Where's Maggie?" he asked.

"Upstairs in her room," said Mom. "She hasn't been herself today. She was running around earlier with no clothes on!"

"Maggie?" Dad called, running up the stairs. "Where's my little girl?" He opened her bedroom door. Of course, Maggie wasn't there.

And she wasn't a little girl, either. At that moment, Maggie was a

floppy-eared bunny rabbit with a
chameleon on her back. And she
was galloping, flippity floppity down

the street with a large, slobbery dog
snapping at her heels!

The dog was called Rufus. He had
always been her friend when she was
Maggie the witch. But now that she
was Maggie the bunny, he seemed
determined to gobble her up!

Maggie didn't know which way
to turn and was about to dash out
into the road when Bat decided to
take control. He grabbed Maggie's
long ears and used them to steer
her. He pulled her left ear to avoid
a passing cyclist, and her right ear

to steer around a pile of dog poop.
Then, suddenly, he pulled both ears
together. Maggie skidded to a stop
right next to a small gap in the fence.
They dived through it just in time!

Rufus was too big to get through
the gap. He was left behind, barking

furiously, as Maggie and Bat ran off across the park and into the woods beyond.

Maggie and Bat flopped down, panting on the leafy ground. They looked around them. It was very dark under the trees and they could hear something moving in the bushes. What if it was a hungry fox who fancied a bunny for dinner and a chameleon for dessert?

Maggie gulped. She didn't know what to do. She was cold, tired, sad, scared and lost. Bat didn't know which color to change to first!

Then it started to rain.

Maggie's floppy ears drooped, her pink nose twitched and big bunny teardrops splashed onto Bat, who was now clinging to her furry tummy.

Suddenly, in the distance, they saw a tiny light glowing in the dark.

Maggie made a noise that sounded like a squeak, but was probably "Yikes! It's a fox! A fox with one eye!" in rabbit language.

But it wasn't a hungry one-eyed fox. It was a firefly.

Then there was another and another, until the woods were speckled with hundreds of magical fireflies lighting a path.

Bat thought that the fireflies
looked rather tasty and caught two
or three with his long tongue as they
hopped deeper into the woods.

Following the glowing path,
Maggie and Bat arrived at a clearing
where a lopsided building huddled
under the trees. It had a tower on
one side, a rather crooked chimney
on the other, and soft orangey light
shining from its windows.

Maggie beamed a big bunny smile.
It was Grandpa Sparks' cottage! She
hurried to the door and scratched
at it with her claws. Bat climbed
up and dangled from the doorbell,

making it ring over
and over again.

Back at home, Mom and Dad were worried. They had looked everywhere for Maggie: behind the couch, under the table, in the shower, on top of the wardrobe, even under the sink.

"Maggie, where are you?" called Mom in a panic.

"Hetty! In here! Quick!" called Dad from Maggie's bedroom. "Look, it's Maggie's wand."

"Oh no!" cried Mom. "What if Maggie's been doing magic? Anything could have happened!"

"We'd better go and look for her!" said Dad, strapping Alfie to his chest

in a baby sling. Alfie was still crying,
but as soon as they went outside,
he stopped.

"BUM BUM!"

he shouted.

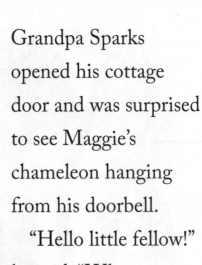

Chapter 5

Grandpa Sparks opened his cottage door and was surprised to see Maggie's chameleon hanging from his doorbell.

"Hello little fellow!" he said. "What are you doing here? Where's Maggie?"

Bat pointed his tail at the doorstep.
Grandpa Sparks looked down to see
a rather soggy bunny looking back
at him.

"Oh dear! Is that you, Maggie
Moo?"

The bunny nodded.

"Well come on in before you
catch a cold!" said Grandpa Sparks,
hurrying them both inside.

He dried Maggie and Bat with
warm towels, wrapped them up in
blankets and sat them by the fire.
As they sat warming their toes,
Grandpa Sparks rang Maggie's
dad.

"Sorry, I can't talk now," said
Dad. "We can't find Maggie and we
think she's been doing magic! We've
looked all over but there's no sign—"

"She's here!" said Grandpa Sparks.
"Bat's here too."

"OH, THANK GOODNESS!"
gasped Dad.

Then Mom grabbed the phone,
"IS SHE ALRIGHT?"

"Er, well, she seems OK, but she's a bit ..."

"A bit what?" asked Mom.

"A bit ... fluffier than usual," said Grandpa Sparks.

A few minutes later, Mom and Dad burst through the door of Grandpa Sparks' cottage. They couldn't believe their eyes!

Mom kneeled down and gently stroked the soft fur behind Maggie's ears. "Oh, Maggie, why did you turn yourself into a bunny?"

"Bum bum!" cried Alfie,
trying to wriggle out of
his baby sling to reach
Maggie.

"Oh!" laughed Dad. "He didn't want me to change his diaper at all. He was trying to say 'bunny!'"

"Never mind changing nappies," said Grandpa Sparks. "How do we change Maggie back into a little girl?"

"I could try a spell?" said Dad.

"Are you sure, Tom?" asked Mom in a worried voice.

"Of course!" he said, handing her a drool-covered Alfie. "But I'll need a bit more light!"

Dad pointed his wand at the light
bulb and said:

"Sunshine gold
and lightning white,
give us lots
of lovely light!"

POOF!

The spell worked! The light bulb
grew brighter and brighter and
brighter …

"That's enough darling," said Mom.

But Dad didn't know how to stop
the spell. Suddenly …

POP!

All the lights in the house went out.

Dad jumped in surprise and dropped his wand. "Whoops!"

"You are definitely not doing any spells on Maggie," said Mom firmly.

The room was dark now, except for the glow from the fire and an extra glow coming from Bat's tummy.

"Hmm," said Grandpa Sparks, as he reached into the cupboard for some candles. "It looks like someone's been eating my fireflies."

Grandpa Sparks lit
the candles and soon the
room was flickering with
bright golden light.

Grandpa Sparks, Mom and Dad huddled together and talked in whispers (the way grown-ups do when they don't want children to hear what they're saying).

But while the adults were whispering, Alfie was crawling towards Maggie … holding Dad's wand! Alfie sat down beside Maggie, reached out his sticky little hands and gave her a big hug.

"Bye, bye, bum bum," he said.

POOF!

Maggie turned back into a little girl. She had human hands and

human toes and curly human hair
again.

Maggie was so happy to be back to
normal that she hugged Alfie back.

Mom and Dad and Grandpa Sparks rushed over, freed Dad's wand from Alfie's sticky fingers and pulled him and Maggie into a great big group hug.

For the first time in a long time, Maggie felt happy and special and loved. Bat turned a bright, sunshine yellow.

Maybe, thought Maggie, having a baby brother isn't so bad.

PAAAAAAAARP!

Maggie's eyes started watering.

"Ew! Alfieeeee!"